For Grummy and Gargar

SIMON & SCHUSTER
BOOKS FOR YOUNG READERS
Simon & Schuster Building, Rockefeller Center
1230 Avenue of the Americas, New York, New York 10020

Budgie
And the Blizzard

1993
Merry Christmas
Briana !
Love,
your Mommy & Dad's
friends,
Caren, David &
Desirée Miller
in California ♡

H.R.H. The Duchess of York
Illustrated by John Richardson

SIMON & SCHUSTER BOOKS FOR YOUNG READERS
PUBLISHED BY SIMON & SCHUSTER
NEW YORK LONDON TORONTO SYDNEY TOKYO SINGAPORE

It was early December and a cold wind howled through the countryside. In their snug little farmhouse, Mr. and Mrs. Fairweather were putting the finishing touches on the nursery for the new baby they were expecting to be born in a couple of weeks. Mr. Fairweather finished painting the last wall as Mrs. Fairweather arranged a pretty lace coverlet over the baby's cradle.

"It certainly is cold today," said Mrs. Fairweather. "I just hope we don't get any early storms," answered Mr. Fairweather. "The last thing we need is bad weather when we drive to the hospital."

Mr. and Mrs. Fairweather covered the canary cage, fed the dog, Farckle, and settled down for an evening at home and a long night's sleep.

At the hangar where he lived, Budgie, the little helicopter, was napping in the corner.

"Budgie, where are you?" called his friend Pippa, the Piper Warrior plane.

"Budgie!" shouted the loudspeaker. (It wouldn't have been a loudspeaker if it had whispered.) "Budgie!"

When Pippa finally found him, Budgie was just waking up. "Can't you hear? They've been calling you for five minutes," said Pippa. "Radio back quickly."

Budgie called in and received his instructions. "Just a boring parcel pick up," he grumbled. "Thanks for waking me up, Pippa."

"Next time you have a snooze, don't turn your radio off," scolded Pippa, "and go carefully because it looks like it might snow."

Budgie lifted off at twilight and flew north. Just as it was getting dark, he saw the railway tracks and followed them. Soon he saw the station he was looking for in the town at Bradlion. Budgie landed and asked Mr. Chumpy, the station master, for his parcel.

Mr. Chumpy frowned. "The train is late and your package is on the train. You can stay here but it looks like a terrible storm is coming." Budgie decided he would wait.

Back at the airfield it started to snow and Pippa
worried about her friend.

Budgie had never been out overnight in freezing
weather, and Pippa knew he hated the cold.

Budgie sat huddled as the weather changed to a full blizzard.
He could barely see as the snow drifted over him. The night
dragged on. He began to feel very cold.

Early the next morning, even before the sun rose, Mrs. Fairweather woke up with sharp pains in her middle. She nudged her husband. "Michael," she said. "I think the baby is coming a little early."

They both got out of bed, and could hardly believe their eyes when they looked out the window. Everywhere they looked, they could see nothing but white. The fence around their house was buried, their car was buried, and the snow was still falling. They had both slept soundly as the blizzard had raged outside.

"Pack yourself a little bag for the hospital," said Mr. Fairweather, "and I'll go outside and dig the car out."

"Alright," said Mrs. Fairweather, "but do hurry. I don't think it will be very long before the baby arrives."

About fifteen minutes later, Mr. Fairweather came indoors, looking very worried. "I've dug the car out," he explained, "but I can't get the motor to start!"

"Now don't worry. I'll just make a telephone call or two, and I'm sure we'll find a way to get to the hospital on time," Mrs. Fairweather reassured her nervous husband.

Budgie was startled by the call on his radio. "Control to Budgie. We need your help. We have a woman stranded in her house who's about to have a baby. You are the only helicopter available."

Budgie felt frozen, but replied, "Have them put out a signal
and give me directions. I'll call in after I take off."

Budgie tried to start his engine. On his third attempt the engine caught but his rotor blades wouldn't move. He was iced up!

Budgie felt terrible. He tried to cheer himself up with a joke: Budgie can't budge. Ha, Ha, Ha. It didn't work.

Pippa had been listening to her radio, and guessed that Budgie was having problems. She could not take off on the snow-covered runway, but thought she could help Budgie anyway.

Budgie was cold and miserable when Mr. Chumpy approached with a steaming bucket. "Some one called and said you might be frozen up," he said as he climbed on top of Budgie and poured hot water on his rotor.

Budgie was so grateful. He thanked Mr. Chumpy for the only bath he had ever enjoyed, and then quickly lifted off.

The snow had stopped and the sun was rising as Budgie flew
toward the Fairweathers' farm.

He searched below and finally saw what he thought must be the signal,
three pairs of bright red long-johns flapping on the clothes line.

Budgie landed in deep snow right beside the farm house. Mrs.
Fairweather could barely walk as the couple made their way
through the drifts. Finally they were on board and Budgie flew as
fast as he could to the hospital. As the Fairweathers went inside
they waved and called out, "Thank you! We couldn't have made
it without you."

On his way home, Budgie picked up his parcel at the train station. By the time he landed at the hangar, Pippa was so excited she could hardly stand it.

"They had a baby boy," she explained. "They named him Jack B. Fairweather and the B. stands for Budgie!"

Budgie beamed. "I bet I know who suggested a hot bath for me. If they ever have a little girl they should name her Pippa."